Splish, Splash, Ducky!

Lucy Cousins

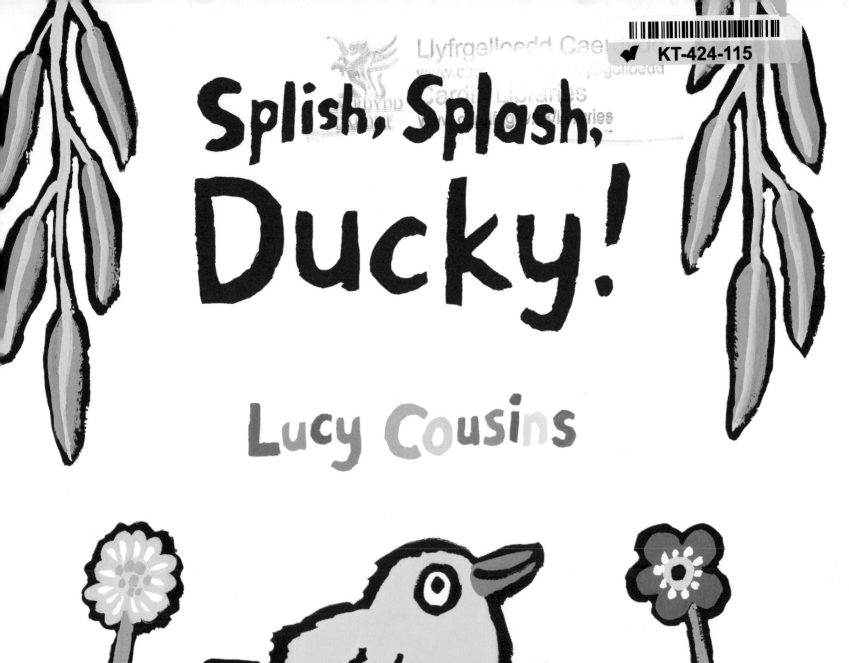

Hello, I am Ducky Duckling!

When I'm feeling happy
I say...

Quack,

quack, quack!

Oh, goody, hooray!
It's raining today.
I'm going to find
my friends to play.

Drip, drip, drop,
I hop with frog.

Quack, quack, quack!

I like to squirm
with wriggly worm.

A hug for bug
and a hug for slug.

Quack, quack, quack!

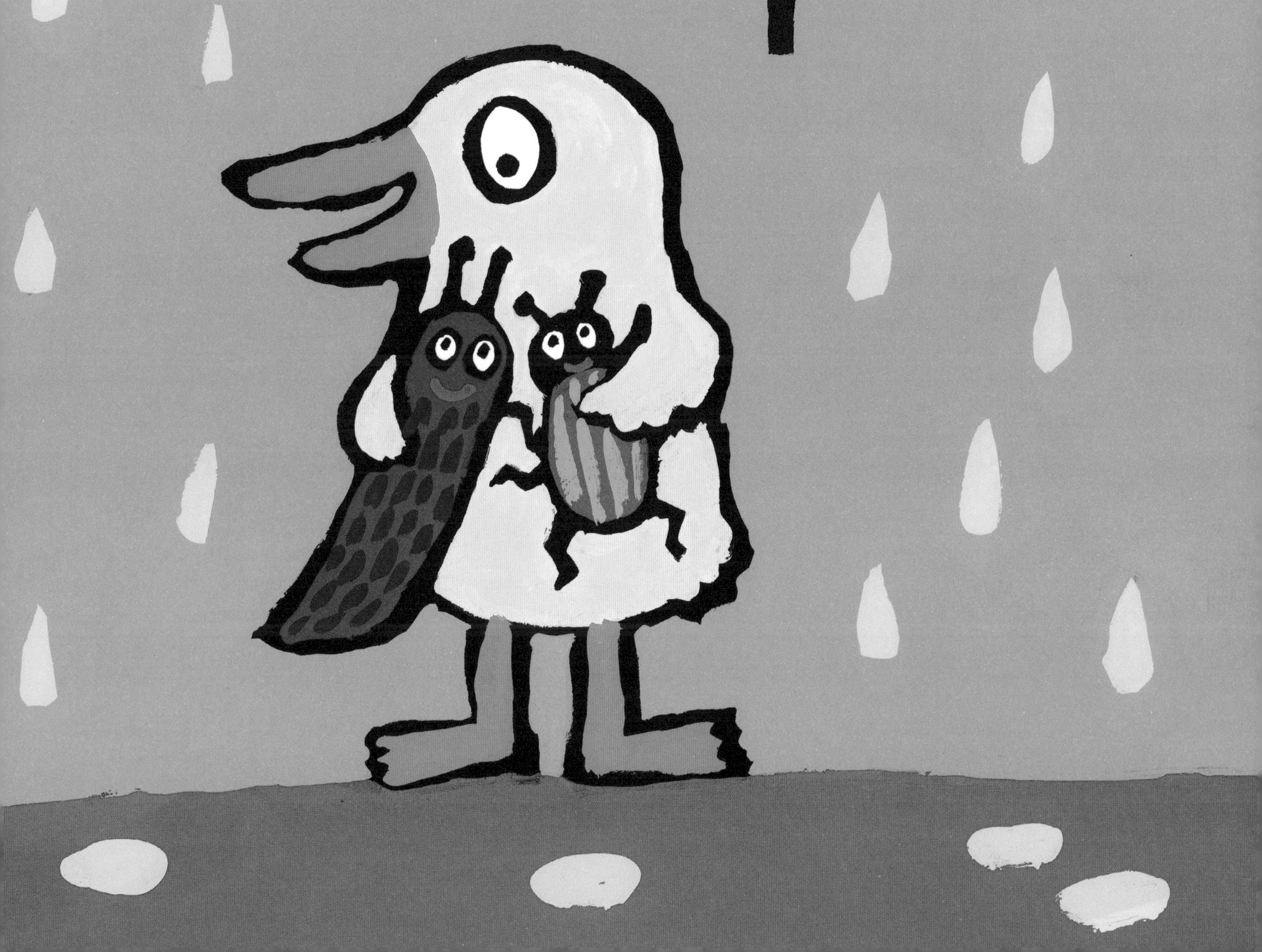

Into the pond
to play with the swans.

Quack,
quack,
quack!

Splash, splish,
I swim with fish.

Quack, quack, quack!

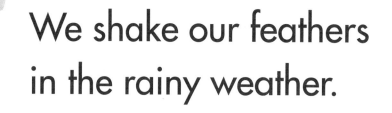

We shake our feathers
in the rainy weather.

Drip, drop, plip, plop.
Rain is funny on your tummy.

Quack,
quack,
quack!

Squeak, squeak,
hide and seek.

Quack,
quack,
quack!

Oh, no!
The rain has stopped.

No more drips.
No more drops.

No more quacking,
I'm feeling sad.
I think I'll go
and see my Dad.

Cheer up Ducky,
here comes the sun.
Look at the butterflies
having fun.

We'll quack together
whatever the weather.
Hop on my back and…

For Gabriel

First published 2018 by Walker Books Ltd
87 Vauxhall Walk, London SE11 5HJ

2 4 6 8 10 9 7 5 3 1

© 2018 Lucy Cousins

The right of Lucy Cousins to be identified as author/illustrator of this work has been
asserted by her in accordance with the Copyright, Designs and Patents Act 1988.

This book has been typeset in Futura.
Handlettering by Lucy Cousins.

Printed in China

British Library Cataloguing in Publication Data:
a catalogue record for this book is available from the British Library.

ISBN 978-1-4063-7679-1

www.walker.co.uk